Bubble Gum

Africa Stories

Bubble Gum
by
Kate Noble

Illustrations
by
Rachel Bass

SILVER SEAHORSE PRESS
Chicago

ISBN 0-9631798-0-2

Manufactured in the United States of America
1   2   3   4   5   6   7   8   9   10

For all the twinkies

with love

Kimbi was a little baboon

who lived in a park in Africa. All

the baboons liked to play at the

camp where the visitors stayed.

The people laughed at the

baboons, but they talked about

lions. They looked for lions to take

pictures of. Kimbi found it tiresome.

Kimbi loved the camp. The

people kept sweets in their tents,

and they were always in a hurry.

They never bothered to close the

tent flaps properly.

When they went to the big

building to eat lunch, Kimbi could

get in and look around.

Today was going to be a good

day. Kimbi saw the smiling woman

leave her tent. He pulled the flap

open and disappeared inside.

He saw it right away. A clear,

crackly bag of things wrapped in pink

paper. He picked it up and, quick as a

wink, he was outside and off to his

favorite spot behind a tree.

The bag made lots of noise when

he opened it. The pink paper was easy

though, and the fat pink stuff inside

was delicious.

Kimbi chewed it. But it didn't

chew up. He ate more of it. And

more. He opened his mouth and a

pink bubble came out. It was so big

Kimbi couldn't see around it.

How unusual!

Kimbi ate lots of sweets, but

they never made bubbles.

Splat! The bubble burst.

Pieces of it stuck to his face. He

pulled on it. It tickled his nose,

and it didn't come off very well.

He scooped up the bag. Time

to go. He'd worry about it later.

After lunch the people went
to the swimming pool. They jumped
into the water and splashed about.

Kimbi climbed to his favorite
branch above the pool. He chewed
some pink stuff. And then some
more. What a nice afternoon this
was turning out to be!

He saw a man turn upside

down in the water and he laughed.

The pink stuff made a bubble again.

This time the bubble was almost

as big as Kimbi. And it grew. Bigger

and bigger. Now it was bigger than

Kimbi. He opened his eyes wide, but

all he could see was the giant bubble.

His head felt light.

He reached for the branch beneath him,

but it wasn't there.

He felt like he was floating.

HE WAS FLOATING.

Higher and higher.

The pink bubble lifted him like a giant balloon.

Kimbi had seen hot-air balloons.

They carried people high over the park

to look at animals.

Lions, of course.

Now he had a balloon of his very own.

When he tilted sideways,

he could just see around the bubble.

He was way up in the sky

above the pool.

What should he do?

Who would help him?

Maybe he would float away forever.

The idea scared him so much that he opened

his mouth and shouted,

"Help."

"Help."

"Help."

Then he heard a pop.

And a splat.

The bubble burst and was all

over him. He was falling. Fast. Pow.

Oh! Was he dead? No. He was wet.

He was in the swimming pool.

And sinking. Baboons don't swim.

People swim. Who was going to help?

A strong arm lifted him to the

surface and pulled him from the water.

It was the man who jumped

into the water upside down.

Kimbi tried to smile, but his face

was stiff. His feet seemed to be stuck.

A woman rushed up.

"Is he all right?" She looked down

at him. "I got a wonderful picture.

There he was, floating through the air

with his own big pink balloon."

A picture? Kimbi had his picture

taken, floating through the air?

Let the lions try that.

The man and the woman

were pulling the pink stuff off.

Ouch. Some hair went with it.

Kimbi knew he had to get

out of here. The camp manager

would chase him. His mother

would scold him. She had warned

him not to go near the people.

He jumped to his feet

and ran. He went round a tree,

then another. He would find

his friends. They would help

him pull the sticky stuff off.

What a story he had to tell them!

About flying.

About getting his picture taken.

About going swimming.